PLATE 1

PLATE 2

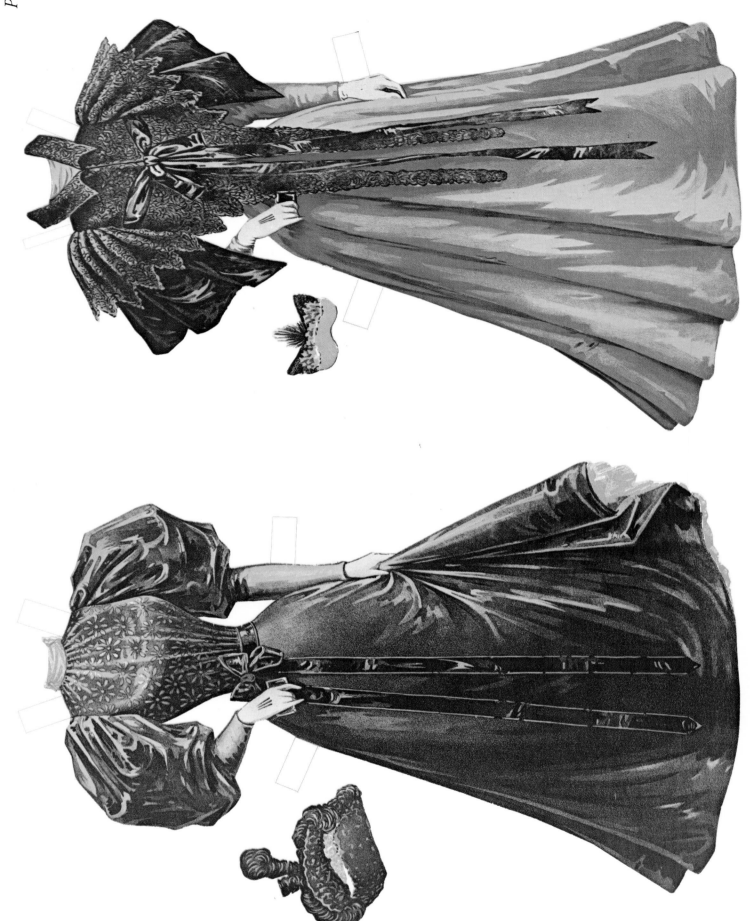

LADIES' COSTUME
April 14, 1895

LADIES' TOILETTE
March 31, 1895

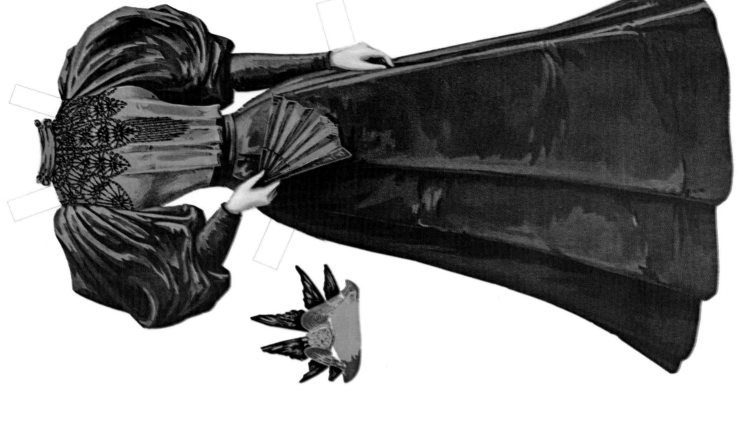

PLATE 3

LADIES' TOILETTE
May 5, 1895

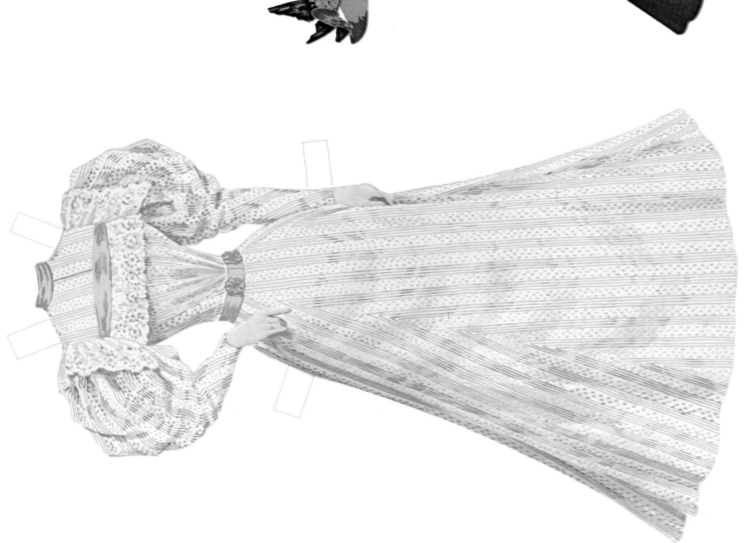

LADIES' SUMMER TOILETTE
April 21, 1895

PLATE 4

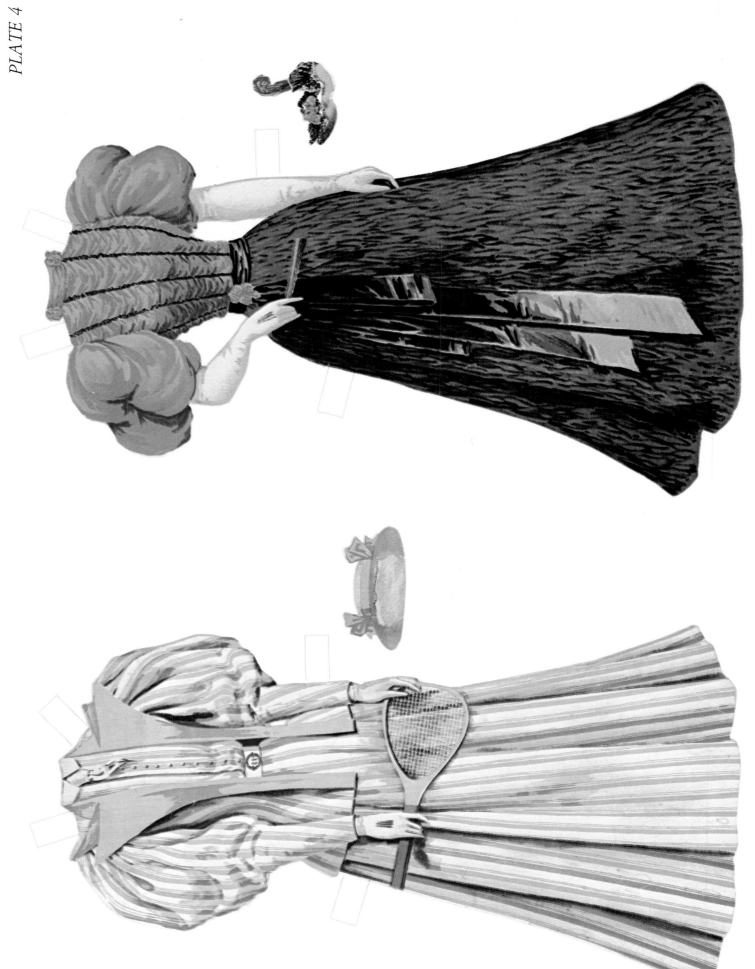

LADIES' EVENING TOILETTE
May 26, 1895

LADIES' OUTING SUIT
May 12, 1895

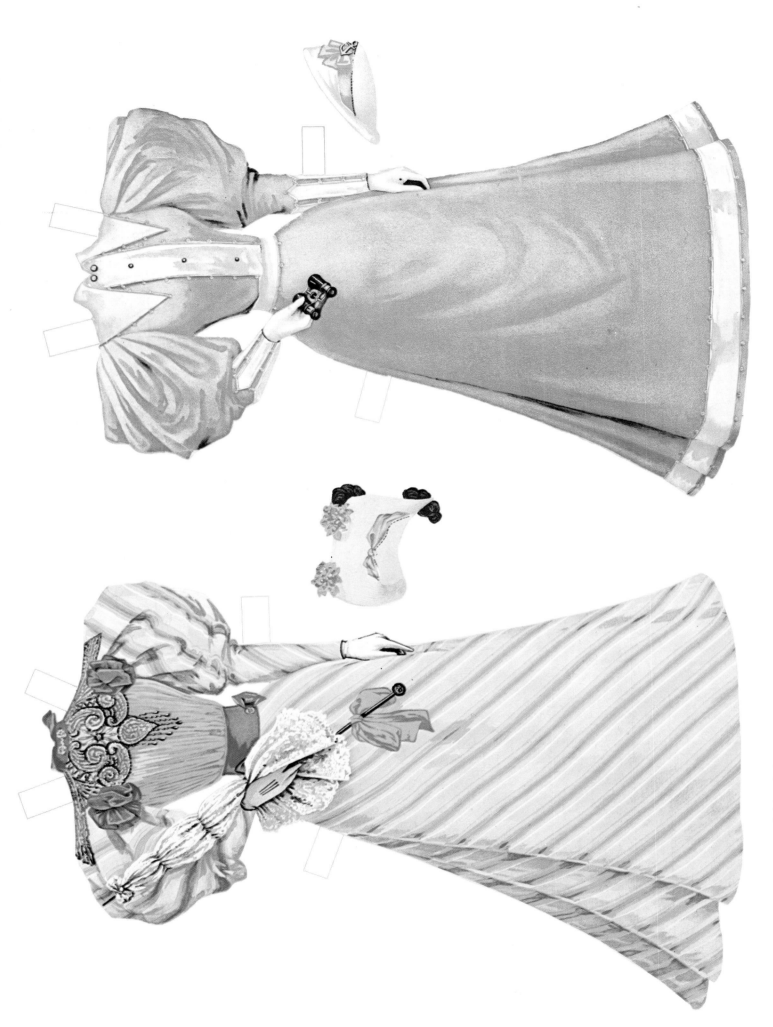

PLATE 5

LADIES' YACHTING TOILETTE
June 9, 1895

LADIES' TOILETTE
June 2, 1895

PLATE 6

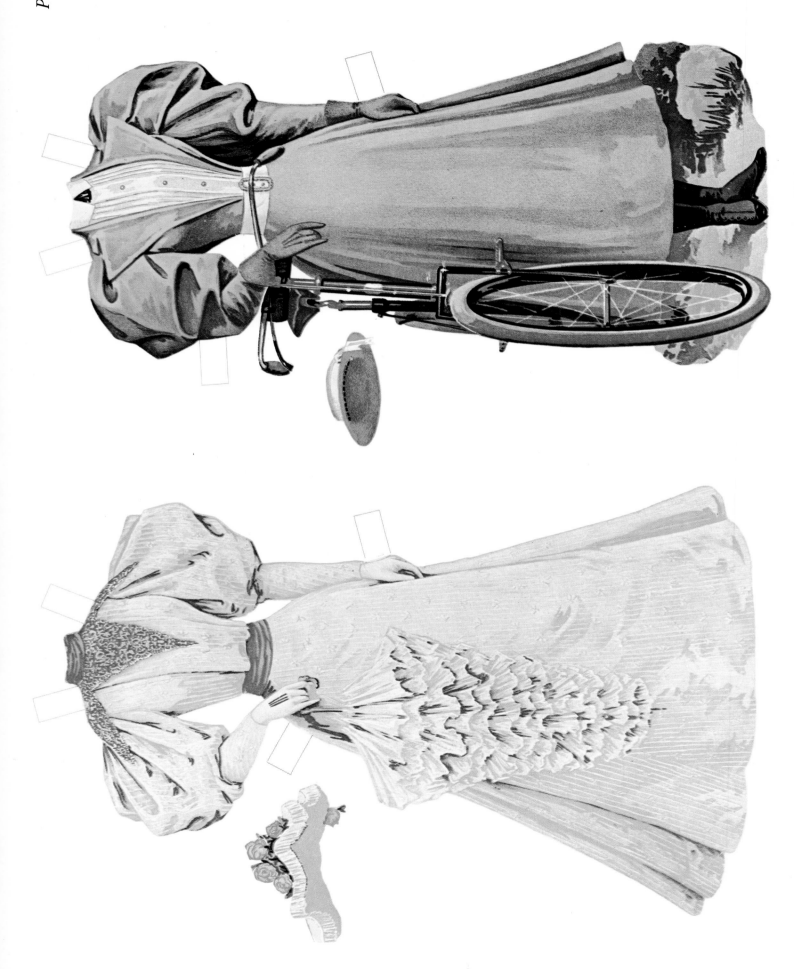

LADIES' BICYCLE COSTUME
June 30, 1895

GARDEN PARTY TOILETTE
June 23, 1895

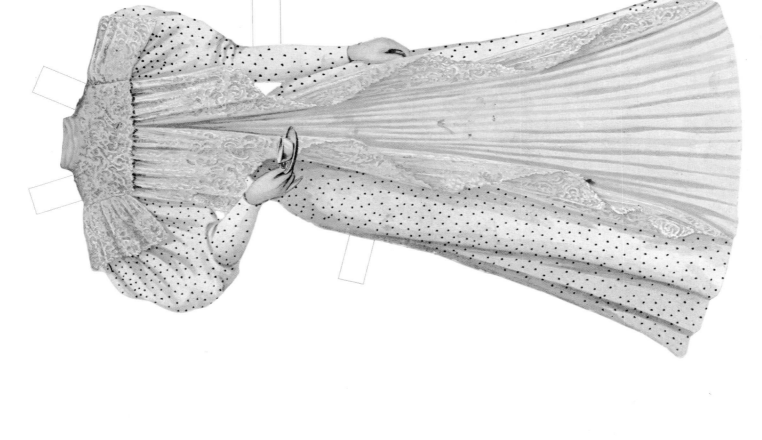

LADIES' TEA GOWN
July 14, 1895

PLATE 7

LADIES' BATHING SUIT
July 7, 1895

PLATE 8

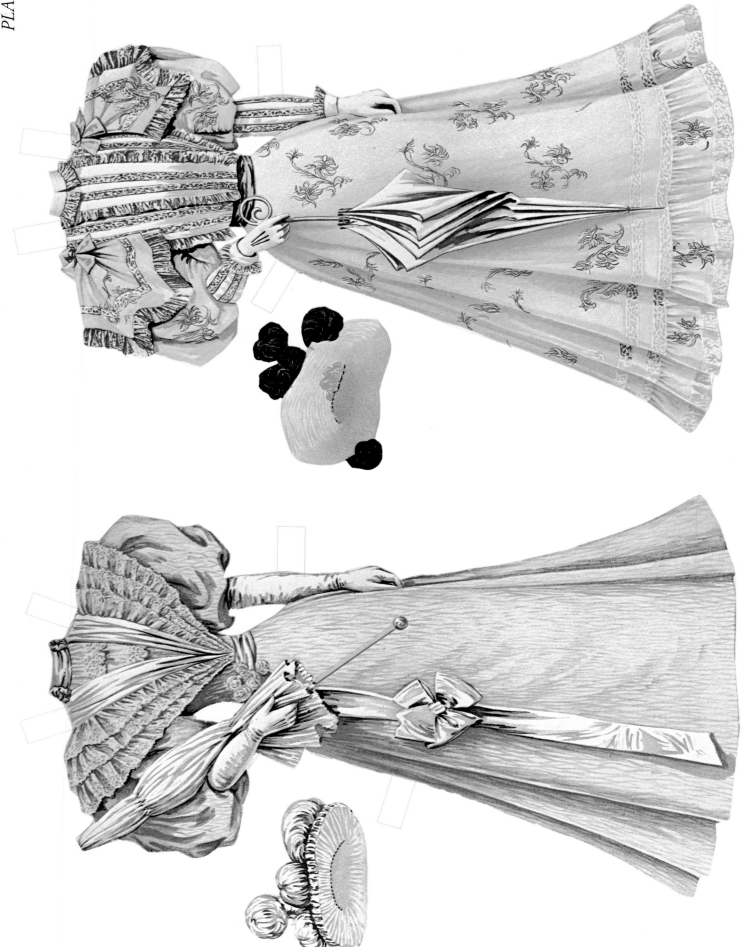

LADIES' CASINO TOILETTE
August 4, 1895

LADIES' SEASIDE TOILETTE
July 28, 1895

WEDDING GOWN
August 25, 1895

LADIES' AFTERNOON TOILETTE
August 11, 1895

PLATE 9

PLATE 10

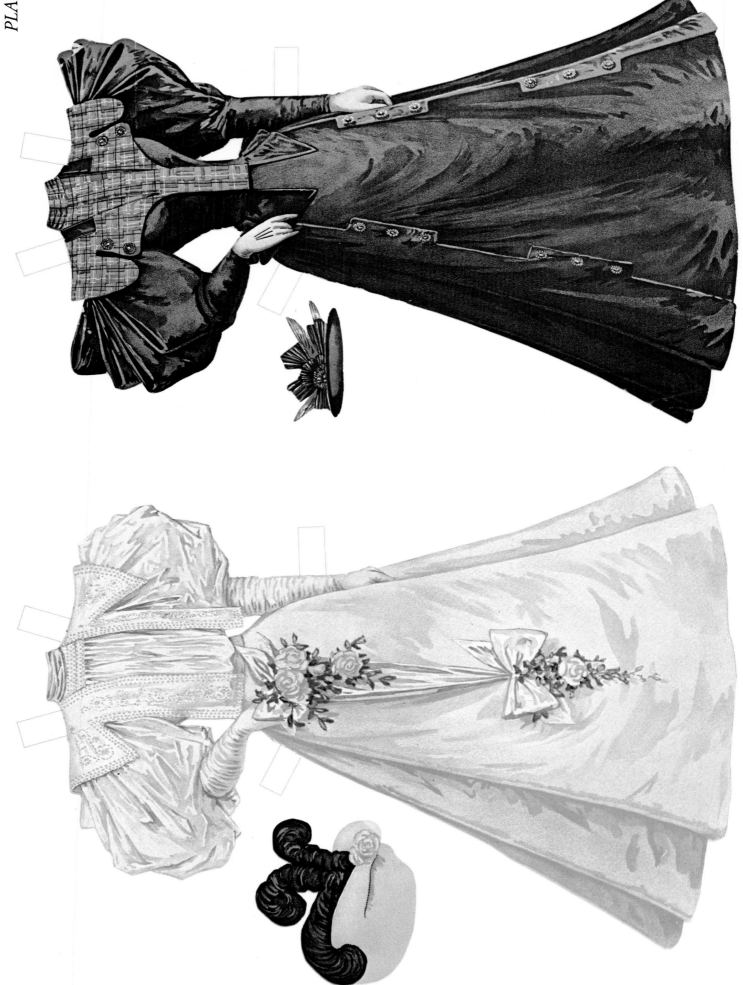

LADIES' WALKING TOILETTE
September 8, 1895

BRIDESMAID'S TOILETTE
September 1, 1895

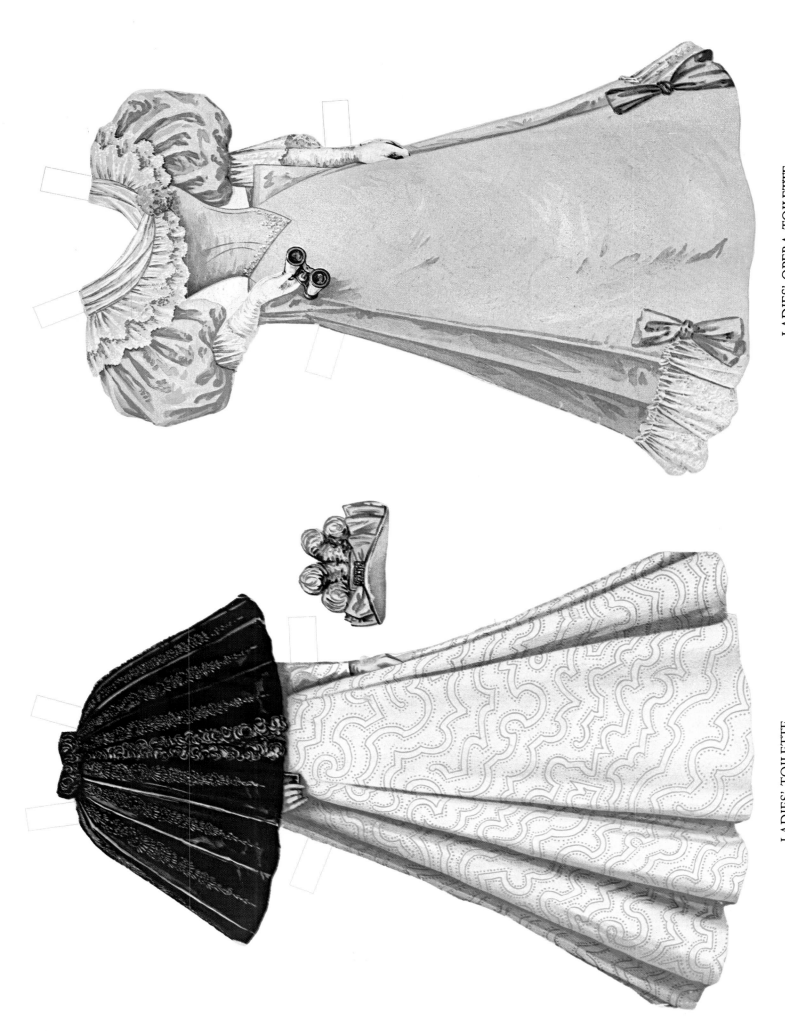

PLATE 11

LADIES' OPERA TOILETTE
September 29, 1895

LADIES' TOILETTE
September 22, 1895

PLATE 12

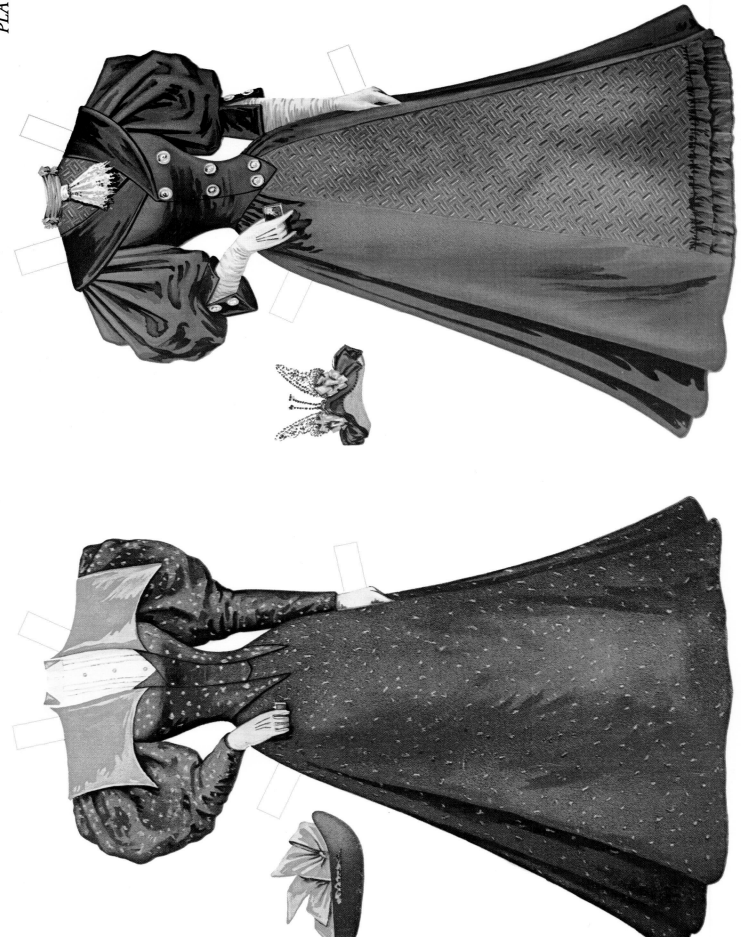

LADIES' REDINGOTE COSTUME
October 13, 1895

LADIES' ENGLISH JACKET SUIT
October 6, 1895

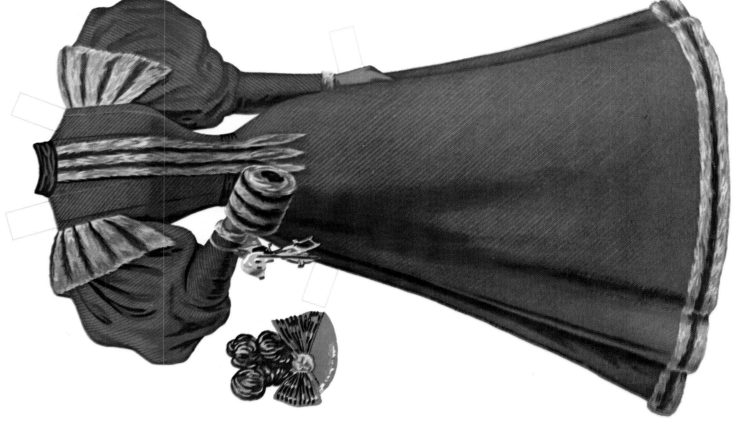

LADIES' SKATING TOILETTE
January 5, 1896

PLATE 13

LADIES' OPERA CLOAK
October 27, 1895

PLATE 14

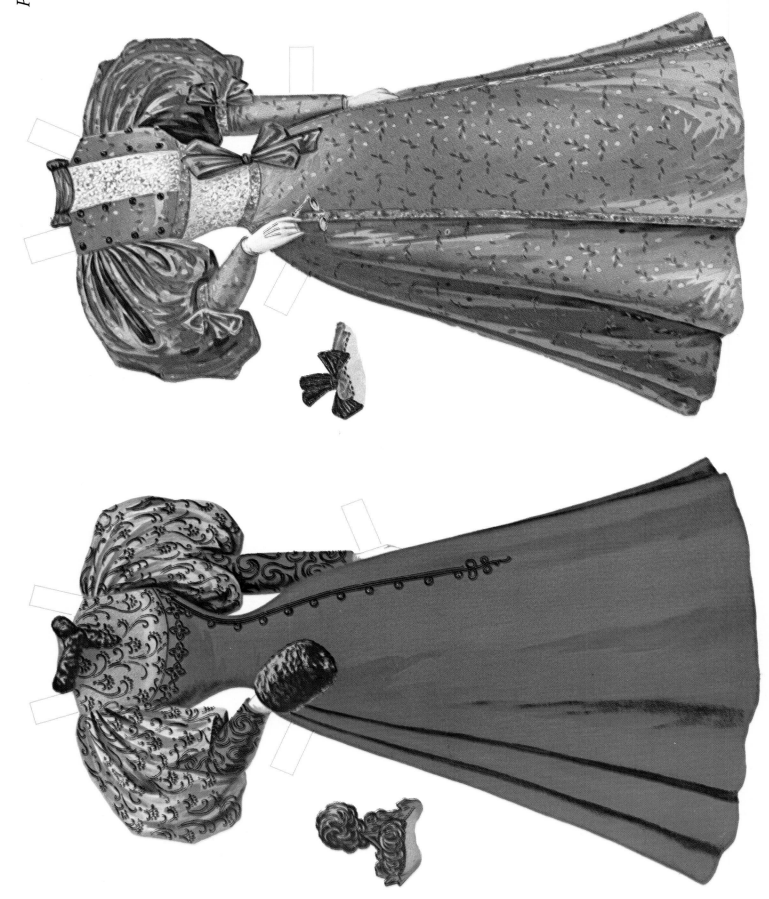

LADIES' LUNCHEON TOILETTE
January 26, 1896

LADIES' PRINCESS TOILETTE
January 19, 1896

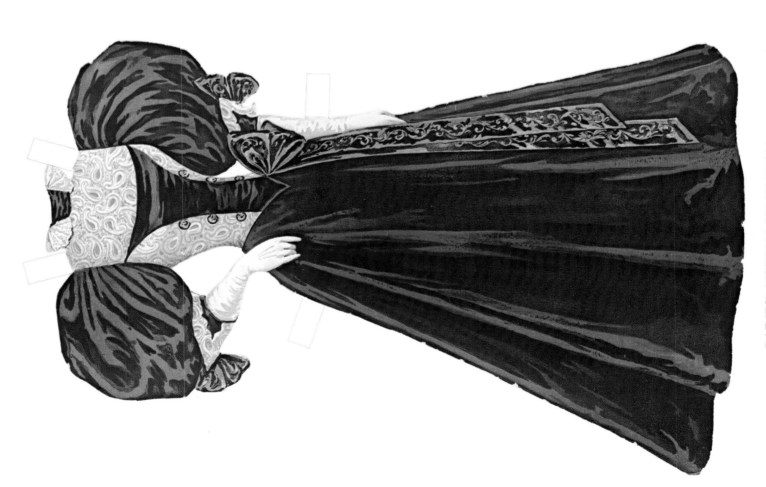

LADIES' CONCERT TOILETTE
February 9, 1896

PLATE 15

LADIES' AFTERNOON TOILETTE
February 2, 1896

PLATE 16

LADIES' DEMI-EVENING TOILETTE
February 23, 1896

LADIES' HOME TOILETTE
February 16, 1896

FROGGY GOES TO THE LIBRARY

FROGGY GOES TO THE LIBRARY

by JONATHAN LONDON

illustrated by FRANK REMKIEWICZ

VIKING

This one's for the librarians (especially Sonoma County librarians)
and specifically for Miss Tiffany—*flop flop flop.*
Oh, and for Ruby, too.
    —J.L.

For Sarabeth Kalajian, Sarasota library leader.
    —F.R.

VIKING
Penguin Young Readers Group
An imprint of Penguin Random House LLC
375 Hudson Street
New York, New York 10014

First published in the United States of America by Viking, an imprint of Penguin Random House LLC, 2016

Text copyright © 2016 by Jonathan London
Illustrations copyright © 2016 by Frank Remkiewicz

LIBRARY OF CONGRESS CATALOGING-IN-PUBLICATION DATA
Names: London, Jonathan, 1947– | Remkiewicz, Frank, illustrator.
Title: Froggy goes to the library / by Jonathan London ; illustrated by Frank Remkiewicz.
Description: New York : Viking, published by Penguin Group, [2016]. |
Series: The Froggy books | Summary: When Froggy, Mom, and Pollywogilina set out
for the library, Froggy brings a wheelbarrow to hold all the books he
plans to borrow but he is so excited that he forgets to use his indoor voice.
Identifiers: LCCN 2015028370 | ISBN 9780670015733 (hardback)
Subjects: | CYAC: Libraries—Fiction. | Behavior—Fiction. | Frogs—Fiction.
| BISAC: JUVENILE FICTION / Animals / Frogs & Toads. | JUVENILE FICTION /
Books & Libraries. | JUVENILE FICTION / Humorous Stories.
Classification: LCC PZ7.L8432 Frj 2017 | DDC [E]—dc23 LC record available at http://lccn.loc.gov/2015028370

Manufactured in China   Set in ITC Kabel Std   These illustrations were made with watercolor

10 9 8 7 6 5 4 3 2 1

It was Saturday morning,
and Froggy stayed in bed
to read his favorite book.
(It was about Super Frog!)

FRROOGGYY!

called his mom.
"Wha-a-a-t?"
"It's time to get up, dear.
We're going to the library!"
"Yippee!" cried Froggy, and he
hopped out of bed
and flopped into the kitchen—
flop flop flop.

"Let's go!" said Froggy,
And he started flopping out the door—
flop flop flop.
"First," said Mom, "you have to get dressed!"
"I know that!" said Froggy,

and he flopped back to his room and got dressed—*zip! zoop! zup! zut! zut! zut! zat!*

Then he flopped back—*flop flop flop*—
and said, "Let's go! I want to get books
about Super Frog and T. rex!"
"But first, eat your breakfast, dear."
"Yum!" said Froggy. "Home flies and ketchup!"—
munch crunch munch.

Then Froggy raced out the door.

FRROOGGYY !

called Mom.
"Wha-a-a-t?"
"Don't forget your book bag, dear,
so you can carry home lots of books!"

"I'd better take the wheelbarrow!" cried Froggy.
"I'm getting tons of books!"

And off to the library they went—
squeak! squeak! squeak!

In no time at all,
Froggy had a stack of books so high
that he couldn't see over the top.

So he tripped over Polly—"Oops!"—
and fell smack on his face—*zplat!*—
and spilled all his books.

And that's when he saw Frogilina.
"Hi, Froggy!" *Hee-hee!*
"Want some help picking up your books?"
"I CAN DO IT MYSELF!" shouted Froggy.
"Please use your indoor voice, dear,"
said the librarian, Miss Otterbottom.

First, Froggy read a book
about Super Frog.
(He wasn't very good at
reading, but he was very good at
looking at the pictures.) *Zwit! zwit!*

When he got to the part
about Super Frog
flying high and fast after the bad guys,
he stood on the table
and spread his arms like wings . . .

Then he picked out lots of books about dinosaurs—especially his favorite: T. rex.

ROOAARRR!

cried Froggy,
holding his hands up like claws.

FRROOGGYY!

called Miss Otterbottom.
"Wha-a-a-a-t?"
"This is a library, dear.
Not Dinosaur Park!"
"Oops!" said Froggy.
"Sorry."

Then Miss Otterbottom announced,
"Storytime! Come gather around, children!"
"Me! Me!" cried Pollywogilina.
"Storytime is for babies!" said Froggy.

But little by little, the book that Miss Otterbottom was reading got all of his attention.

What a great story! thought Froggy.
And he wanted to know what happened next,
so he scooted closer . . . and closer . . .

and when she started doing rhymes
and songs, he got so excited
that he leapfrogged over Frogilina . . .
he leapfrogged over his mother . . .
he leapfrogged over Polly . . .

right smack beside Miss Otterbottom,
and started singing:
   "Wiggle wiggle! Waggle waggle!
    Giggle giggle! Gaggle gaggle!"
And the kids all laughed like crazy
and Froggy kept singing and dancing—

until suddenly it grew quiet.
So quiet you could hear a fly burp.
Froggy took one look at Miss Otterbottom
and—*uh-oh*—he knew he was in trouble.

"Oops!" cried Froggy, looking more red
in the face than green.
Miss Otterbottom stared hard at him . . .

then smiled and joined in—
and so did everybody else—
"Wiggle wiggle! Waggle waggle!
Giggle giggle! Gaggle gaggle!"—
until storytime was over.

"Thanks for being so, uh,
energetic, Froggy!" said Miss
Otterbottom.
And she handed him the book
she had been reading aloud,
and said,
"I'm glad to know that
Froggy loves books!
Come again soon!"

"Thanks!" cried Froggy.
"Books are the best!"
And he put it on top of his pile
to check out . . .

then rolled his wheelbarrow full of books—
with Polly on top, singing,
"Wiggle wiggle! Waggle waggle!
Giggle giggle! Gaggle gaggle!"—

all the way home—
squeak! squeak! squeak!